Eric a[nd the]
Peculiar Pong

Other TIGERS by Barbara Mitchelhill

Eric and the Striped Horror

Eric and the Wishing Stone

Eric and the Pimple Potion

Eric and the Green-Eyed God

Eric and the Voice of Doom

*Damian Drooth, Supersleuth: The Case
of the Disappearing Daughter*

*Damian Drooth, Supersleuth: The Case of
the Pop Star's Wedding*

The Great Blackpool Sneezing Attack

Eric and the Peculiar Pong

BARBARA MITCHELHILL

Illustrated by Bridget MacKeith

Andersen Press • London

First published in 2003 by
Andersen Press Limited,
20 Vauxhall Bridge Road, London SW1V 2SA
www.andersenpress.co.uk

British Library Cataloguing in Publication Data
available
ISBN 1 84270 288 2

Phototypeset by Intype Libra Ltd
Printed and bound in Great Britain by
Mackays of Chatham Ltd.,
Chatham, Kent

Chapter 1

Eric was trying to become invisible at the back of the hall. Miss Borrage was picking people to sing solos in the school play, which was 'The Bandits of Old Mexico'. He definitely didn't want to sing by himself – not in front of the Mayor, all the School Governors and Mr Botherington, the chairman. No. He would hide away in the chorus, thank you.

The main parts were already sorted. Annie Barnstable (the worst girl in the class) was going to be the Bandit Queen. She was really chuffed.

Brent Dwyer was Bernardo, the Big Bully Bandit. Was that type-casting or what? thought Eric.

He and Wesley, his best mate, were chosen to be Mexican Bandits. That was cool. There were twenty Bandits so they could merge with the rest without anyone noticing them in particular.

Miss Borrage was busy writing it all down on her notepad. 'Now I need someone to sing one of the verses in the final song,' she said looking around. 'Put up your hand if you are one of the Bandits.'

Eric made himself as short as possible by bending his knees. Then he raised his hand slowly and kept it close to his chest. That way he hoped she wouldn't notice him. But he was wrong.

Miss Borrage scanned the forest of hands as they waved eagerly but her gaze finally landed on Eric. She smiled her gorgeous smile. Her big blue eyes fixed on him like a laser beam.

'Ah, Eric,' she said. 'Your band won the Junior Pop competition last

term, didn't it? You're almost a pop
star. You'll be perfect. You'll do it,
won't you?'

He couldn't turn her down. He
nodded helplessly and said, 'OK.'

Straight away, his stomach filled
with a terrible churning. He should
have said no. He knew it.

'Miss Borrage thinks I can sing just
because I was in a band,' Eric
complained to Wesley at dinner time.
'But I didn't sing by myself. We all
sang at once, didn't we, Wez? Nobody
could tell how bad I was, really.'

'You sounded OK, Ez.'

Eric shook his head.

'It was the microphone. It made my voice sound loads better. It's not much more that a pathetic squeak really.'

'Nobody could tell.'

'But we don't have mikes in our school plays.'

'You can work on your singing, Ez,' said Wesley, trying to cheer him up. 'You've got two weeks to practise. You'll be OK.'

'I'll be hopeless,' said Eric. 'It'll be a nightmare, singing to a hall full of grown-ups. And the Mayor and all the School Governors will be there, for sure. It can't get any worse than that.'

The thought of it was too much. He was already fed up with the snide remarks and titters from some of the other kids – mainly Annie Barnstable and Brent Dwyer.

'Just think, Ez,' Wesley said, beaming widely. 'When it's all over, it'll be the summer holidays . . . and guess where we're going?'

'Where?'

'America! Disneyland, probably.'

Eric forgot about his singing voice. Suddenly, he was green with envy. He had always wanted to go to Disneyland.

'Don't think we're going away this year,' he said. 'Mum's so ratty she won't ever talk about it. She says we can't go because of the baby.'

'Typical,' said Wez. 'There's always an excuse.'

Eric and Wez sat and stared into the distance.

'I don't know what's wrong with her these days,' said Eric. 'She used to cook me brilliant breakfasts and see that my PE kit was packed and everything. Not now. She's always saying she's tired.'

Wez nodded sympathetically.

'I don't know what she does all day,' Eric continued. 'She's only got the baby to look after and go down to the supermarket. I ask you. How difficult is that?'

'Could you do something to snap her out of her moods?' Wesley suggested.

'Like what?'

'Dunno.'

They sat in silence. Nothing came. No solutions. Nothing. Then Eric remembered it was Mum's birthday the following Saturday. This could be a real chance to cheer her up.

'The Bodge is going to cook her a special meal,' said Eric. (The Bodge was his new stepdad and his old class teacher – very embarrassing.) 'I could make her a cake. I know how to use the electric whisk.'

Wez remembered the first time Eric used the electric whisk. It had taken hours to clean up the kitchen – mainly the walls.

'That's boring, Ez,' said Wesley. 'But we could do a turn?'

'How d'you mean?'

'You know. A cabaret act. Dancing

and singing round the table while they eat. 'I've seen it on the telly.'

Eric chewed his bottom lip. 'Not so keen on the dancing, Wez.'

But Wesley was enthusiastic. 'We could dress up and play our guitars. That would be cool. She'll love it.'

Eric couldn't think of anything better. So he agreed. If Mum was ever going to cheer up, this was probably the way to do it.

Chapter 2

'What we need,' said Wesley, 'are special outfits. We can't do a turn dressed like this.'

Eric agreed.

That afternoon, they bunked off during PE and went down to the stock room where Mrs Cracker, the head teacher, stored the costumes for the school plays. There were boxes of angels' wings and shepherds' headgear – but they wouldn't do. Then Eric saw a box marked 'Bandits of Old Mexico'.

'They must be the costumes for the end of term play,' he said.

They took the lid off and looked inside.

'Brilliant!' said Eric. 'Mexican outfits. Loads of them. Nobody will notice if we borrow a couple of those poncho things.'

'And the hats,' said Wesley.

They squashed two ponchos and two huge sombreros into their sports bags and left them in the cloakroom until home time. It was all fixed.

They called themselves the Tex-Mex

Two and practised every day until Mum's birthday. They even wrote a special song.

Then, on the day itself, Mum said Eric could stay over at Wesley's house. This fitted in brilliantly with Eric's cunning plan.

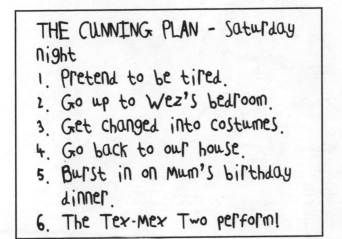

THE CUNNING PLAN - Saturday night
1. Pretend to be tired.
2. Go up to Wez's bedroom.
3. Get changed into costumes.
4. Go back to our house.
5. Burst in on Mum's birthday dinner.
6. The Tex-Mex Two perform!

All went well. They even took gravy granules upstairs, mixed them with water and smeared the mixture over their faces and arms. Earlier in the day, they had made moustaches from bits of Wesley's sisters' hair (in exchange for sweets) and they stuck them on with Superglue to make sure they didn't fall off.

'Cool!' said Eric, looking in the mirror. 'No one will guess they aren't

the real thing. Mum probably won't recognise us.'

By 8 o'clock, Wez's mum and dad were watching TV. Wez's sisters were

fast asleep. The Tex-Mex Two wriggled out of the bedroom window onto the flat roof of the extension. Then they shinned down the drainpipe. Easy.

It was raining heavily as they walked down the street, clutching their guitars.

'These sombreros are better than umbrellas,' said Eric.

It was true. The huge Mexican hats kept most of the rain off them. But it was bad luck that some drops landed on their arms and made the gravy mixture run in streaks onto the ponchos. Still . . . never mind.

When they arrived at Eric's house, they went in by the back door. They crept through the kitchen and into the hall. Everywhere was quiet except for some soppy music coming from the living room.

The door was open a crack, so Eric leaned forward and looked in. Sitting at the table was Mum, wearing a new pink frock. Opposite her was The Bodge, wearing a stripy shirt and looking gooey eyed. There was a cloth on the table (not plastic, like usual) and flowers (real) and candles (pink). A bit over-the-top, Eric thought.

'Ready?' he hissed.

Wez nodded.

Eric flung open the door and leapt inside followed by Wez who strummed his guitar violently. Mum spun round.

'Eric!' she gasped. 'What . . . ?'

The disguise hadn't fooled her but there was still the song to come.

Mama, Mama, Mama,
Your birthday time is here,
Mama, Mama, Mama,
There's nothing much to fear.
You know you're getting older,
So please don't be upset,
Mama, Mama, Mama,
You're the best a kid can get.

On the last note (which didn't sound as good as usual), Eric flung his arms wide and bowed. As he did so, his hat shot off, knocking over the wine and covering Mum's dress with a serious red stain.

She screamed.

Wesley jumped.

His poncho flapped against the candle and it flew across the table, setting fire to a paper napkin.

The Bodge shouted.

Upstairs, the baby cried.

Mum burst into tears.

It was a disaster.

Waaaaaaahhhh!!!

Chapter 3

They ran back to Wesley's house, only to find his parents waiting at the front door.

'We've just been over to Eric's,' panted Wesley. 'We went to wish his mum Happy Birthday.'

'We know,' said his dad gravely. 'She rang.'

According to Mum, they had behaved like hooligans. Eric was put out. Was it his fault that the wine spilled? Or that the candle fell over? No! These things happen. Couldn't Mum see that?

'She snaps at the smallest things these days,' said Eric as he lay in the bunk bed.

'You're right, Ez,' said Wesley. 'Seems unreasonable to make a fuss like that.'

Eric puffed out his cheeks. 'We used to watch TV and have Chinese takeaways. Now all she does is look after the baby and get bad tempered.'

They lay there, their eyes open, looking at the darkness.

'I've been through it, Ez,' said Wesley. 'Kids have a tough time, you know. I can't wait till I get older and things get easier.'

'Yeah,' said Eric and they both turned over and went to sleep.

The next morning, a black cloud hung over Eric's head. He dreaded going home. His life wouldn't be worth living. He decided to sneak up to his room and stay there – for days, if necessary.

He slipped through the front door and was heading for the stairs when Mum called out, 'Eric! Is that you?'

He stopped dead in his tracks. He was doomed.

'Come in the kitchen,' she said – but she didn't sound mad. In fact, she sounded quite happy. She was humming. That was always a good sign.

Cautiously, he pushed open the kitchen door. Mum was standing by the sink. As he walked in, she rushed towards him, flung her arms wide and hugged him. He almost suffocated.

'That was a lovely idea for my birthday, Eric,' she said. 'Shame it went a bit wrong – but never mind, duck. Sit down and I'll make you some breakfast.'

Then she started singing as she put the bacon in the pan. It was just like the old days but Eric noticed that she smelled of something peculiar.

'Do you like my new perfume, Eric?' she said as she poured him a glass of orange.

Eric sniffed. 'Er. Very nice.' He thought he'd better say that, just to be on the safe side.

There was a small bottle on the table and a letter next to it. He knew from the writing that it was from Auntie Rose in South America.

Dear Christine,

Happy Birthday! This perfume is especially for you. It's made locally from the bark of the lixi-lixi tree, which they say is magical. The old man who gave it to me said that it would make you sing with happiness. What a nice thought! I hope you like the smell.

With love to Eric, Brian and baby Rose. Your crazy sister, Rose XXXX

Eric knew that, up until now, Auntie Rose's presents had caused terrible problems. He remembered the Wishing Stone and the Green-eyed God.

30

He couldn't bear to think about them. The Pimple Potion had been really embarrassing. But then there was always a chance this time it would be different.

As it turned out, he was right and things improved rapidly. Mum even offered to take Eric to the pictures.

'I know you want to see "The Third Planet",' she said. 'So we'll leave the baby with Brian and go to see it. Wesley can come, if he likes.'

Eric was really pleased. Everybody at school was desperate to see 'The Third Planet'.

It was no surprise that, when they arrived at the Multiplex, some of the kids from his class were in the ticket queue. Brent Dwyer was there with his brothers. Then Annie Barnstable came through the swing doors. She stood behind him, giggling with two other girls from his class. A large woman with a tight mouth and bright red lipstick stood with them, holding a purse. Probably her gran.

The queue shuffled forward. Soon they had their tickets and were heading for Screen 3. It wasn't until they were settled in their seats that they noticed Brent and his brothers were sitting behind them. Not only that, but Annie Barnstable, her friends and her gran, were in the row in front.

'Just my luck!' said Eric. 'I'm surrounded.'

Not long after the film had started, Mum started fanning herself with an old envelope. 'It's really warm in here,' she said. 'I don't think the air conditioning's working.' She took off her cardigan and stuffed it under her seat.

'I'm boiling,' said Eric and he pulled his sweatshirt over his head.

Wesley did the same. It didn't get any cooler and Mum reached into her handbag, pulled out Rose's perfume and dabbed it behind her ears.

'That's better,' she said.

But as they relaxed to enjoy the film again, a strange thing happened. Mum began to hum under her breath. Obviously, she was enjoying the music on the soundtrack. At first the humming was quiet, but it grew louder and heads began to turn. Brent Dwyer poked Eric in the back.

'Hey, Braithwaite. Tell your mum to stop that noise.'

Eric slid down in his seat. So did Wez.

Mum swivelled round defiantly. 'Noise?' she said to Brent Dwyer. 'That was humming, silly boy. I was just tuning up.'

To Eric's embarrassment, she began to sing along to the soundtrack. Her voice was louder than he had ever heard it before.

Annie Barnstable's gran turned and
prodded her with an umbrella. 'Sssh!'
she hissed. 'You're spoiling the film.'

Everyone in the cinema was looking
in their direction. More people said,
'Sssh!' but Mum wouldn't stop
singing.

By then, Eric and Wez were dying of
shame. They slid off their seats and hid
underneath just as the attendant
arrived with her torch.

'I'm sorry, madam,' she said. 'We've
had several complaints. I must ask you
to leave.'

Chapter 4

It didn't seem to worry Mum that she had been thrown out of the pictures. At her age, too!

'We'll get an ice cream,' she said, 'and then we'll catch the bus. I'll treat you to a three-scoop cornet as it's almost my birthday.'

The ice-cream stall was in the foyer of the Multiplex Cinema. There was a big freezer cabinet with twelve different flavours of ice cream. Eric and Wesley were well pleased at the thought of having three scoops. It made the difficult decision of what to choose, slightly easier.

While they stood there deciding which ones to have, Mum was chatting to the assistant.

'We had a power cut earlier,' he was explaining. 'The air conditioning isn't working.'

Mum smiled and flapped her hand in front of her face. 'I bet you're selling a lot of ice cream,' she said. 'It's so hot – even out here.'

Mum opened her bag and pulled out the bottle of perfume. She squirted it behind her ears. 'Mmmm,' she said, closing her eyes briefly. 'Cool as a cucumber.' And she put the bottle back.

The man turned to Eric who was ready to order his cornet.

'Chocolate Chip and Marshmallow . . . Blueberry Swirl . . . and Banana and Toffee Crunch, please.'

'I'll have the same,' said Wesley.

The ice creams were so big they were sliding off the cones.

'Thanks, Mrs Braithwaite,' said Wesley as they walked to the bus stop. 'This is amazing.'

'I like the Chocolate Chip and Marshmallow best,' said Eric. 'Have a lick, Mum.'

As he turned towards her, he noticed that she was humming a tune under her breath.

'Thanks, duck,' she said, 'but we'll have to run. The bus is coming.'

They got to the bus stop just in time and climbed on board. The bus was almost full but there were some empty seats at the back. It was as they were walking towards them that Mum suddenly exploded into song. Very loudly.

'Here we go! Here we go! Here we go!'

The words rattled against the sides of the bus. Kids looked up and

grinned. Men dropped their
newspapers in surprise. Women
lowered their books and raised their
eyebrows.

Mum carried on alone but soon the
kids joined in. They were the first.
There were about five of them. Then
one or two women started to sing.
Then the bus driver. Before long, the
whole bus was singing. It was just like
a school trip.

When they got home, Eric said, 'Mum, you've got to stop using that perfume.'

'Why should I do that, duck?' she said. 'It's nice.'

'No! It's embarrassing. It makes you sing. One squirt and you're away.'

She looked down at him and smiled. Eric knew she didn't believe him.

He tried again. 'Auntie Rose said that lixi-lixi tree was magic.'

'There's no such thing as magic,

duck. I've just got a voice that has suddenly developed. It's unusual, I know – but there you are. I might seriously think about going into show business.'

'Anyway, that perfume stinks. It's got a peculiar pong!' He said in a feeble attempt to persuade her not to use it. 'I think it's YUK!'

But she still took no notice. She just started clearing the table, singing as she did so.

After that, Eric kept a diary to record 'singing incidents' and gave them stars for embarrassment.

Monday: In supermarket. *

Tuesday: When Mr Botherington, the Chairman of the School Governors called. ***

Wednesday: Outside School. ************

Day by day, it got worse – although Mum wasn't miserable like she used to be. In fact, she was so cheerful that one afternoon Eric dared to mention holidays. Mum was ironing in the kitchen and baby Rose was asleep. It seemed like a good time.

'Mum,' he said. 'Are we going on holiday this year?'

She smiled but didn't say a word.

Just for good measure, he added, 'Wez is going to America.'

45

She looked up. 'Ah, America . . . Hollywood . . . One day I'll go there, duck. I'll be a star. You'll be so proud of me.'

Eric sighed. What was the point? He would never get a sensible answer! He went up to his room and sat on his bed. When, he wondered, would he ever live a normal life?

Chapter 5

As the days passed, Eric got so used to Mum's singing, he stopped worrying about it. When Brent Dwyer had a go at him – 'Your mum's a crazy woman. You'd better keep your eye on her.' – Eric took no notice.

Annie Barnstable told all the girls about the incident at the cinema and they laughed at him – even then, he didn't bother. He had more important things on his mind. In a few days' time, he would have to sing the verse of 'We are the Bandits bold and brave' in front of a hall full of strangers. That was what was bothering him.

'What if my throat dries up? What if my voice gives up on me? I'll feel a right pancake,' he said to Wesley who didn't see the problem.

'You'll be OK, Ez,' he said.

That didn't help.

On Friday night, Eric was so nervous that he couldn't sleep. He got out of bed and stood in front of the mirror and tried to sing. It sounded awful. What a pathetic, puny voice.

'Eric,' Mum called from the bathroom. 'Why aren't you asleep?' She had put the baby to bed and was changing into a clean tee shirt.

'I'm practising my song for tomorrow,' Eric called back. 'I'm useless. I wish I didn't have to do it.'

Mum came into his room smelling of the lixi-lixi tree.

'I thought you liked singing,' she said. 'I thought you wanted to be a pop star?'

'Only if I've got a microphone and only if Mr Botherington isn't in the audience.'

She smiled. 'I'll help you, duck,' she said, picking up the paper with the words and music on it. She sang 'We are the Bandits bold and brave' from beginning to end.

'Lovely song,' she said and sang it
again – but louder.

'Join in, duck,' she called as she
started for a third time. Now she
danced round the room, pretending to
be a Mexican Bandit. Up on the
bed. Leaping onto the

chair. Arms flung
wide. There was
no controlling
her.

'I was meant for
the stage,' she said
as she twirled in
front of the

mirror. 'But I didn't get the chance when I was young. Now *you're* going to be the star of the play, Eric.'

'I'm only in the chorus,' he said.

'But you have a *solo*, duck. I'm very proud of you.'

Eric tried to join in with Mum's singing, but it didn't work. His voice sounded like a mouse with tonsillitis. He felt gloomier than ever.

'It's late, Mum,' he said. 'I'm going to bed.'

Mum smiled. 'Quite right,' she said. 'You need a good night's rest if you're to perform at your best tomorrow.'

Eric climbed into bed and closed his

eyes. He tossed and turned for a while.
When he fell asleep, his mind was
filled with nightmares. He saw clearly
all the things that could go wrong.

The next morning he woke up with
a start. Before he was properly awake,
he realised how to solve the problem.
It was obvious.

'The perfume!' he said to himself. He would find it and dab some behind his ears. Just a small amount. Just enough to give him a reasonable voice.

He jumped out of bed, crossed the landing and went into the bathroom.

Sometimes Mum put perfume on the shelf. Not this time. The shelf was empty. He went into her bedroom. It wasn't there either. That could only mean one thing. It was in her handbag.

When he went down to breakfast, Mum wasn't there. The Bodge said she'd gone to the supermarket. (And her bag with her, thought Eric.)

'When will she be back?'

The Bodge smiled. 'Don't worry, Eric,' he said. 'She'll be back in plenty of time for the play.'

'But I've got to be there for two o'clock.' He felt frantic. What if he didn't get his hands on the perfume?

'It's only half past ten, Eric,' The Bodge laughed. 'She'll be here soon.'

But she didn't get back until one o'clock.

'I've got to feed the baby before I can go to the school,' she said as she walked in. 'You go with Eric, Brian. I'll follow on later. I'll be as fast as I can.'

Just as Eric thought all was lost, Mum flung her bag onto the worktop. Then she turned away to pull the buggy through the back door. The Bodge went to help. While nobody was

looking, Eric opened
the handbag and
dipped his hand
inside. His fingers
closed round the small perfume
bottle and his heart began to pound
with excitement. He pulled it out and
quickly squirted perfume behind his
ears. Then he dropped it back into the
bag just as Mum turned round and
looked at him.

'Are you feeling all right, duck?' she
asked. 'You're not nervous or anything,
are you?'

Eric shook his head. 'I'm cool,
Mum,' he said and he walked away,
humming 'We are the Bandits bold
and brave'.

Chapter 6

There was half an hour to go before curtain-up. Eric was suffering from stage fright and was wondering if the perfume would work when he needed it to.

'Are you a bit nervous, Eric?' Miss Borrage asked as she checked his costume. 'You make a wonderful Bandit, you know.'

Eric blushed. Luckily the layer of make-up was so thick that no one would notice.

'I'm cool,' he said, not wanting her to guess that his stomach was leaping somersaults.

'Have a glass of water before you go on stage,' she suggested. 'That always helps.'

Eric shrugged. 'I'm OK.' He walked away with a confident swagger. Unluckily, Brent Dwyer, dressed as Bernardo, the big, bad bully, bumped into him and ruined the effect.

Eric couldn't help worrying about the perfume. Would it work? Did it only work on Mum? If he could find somewhere quiet he could try out his singing voice, then he would know for sure.

'Go to the loos,' said Wez. 'I'll come with you and keep guard.'

They hurried down the corridor and waited outside until they were certain there was no one in there. Wesley kept a lookout at the door while Eric stood in front of the wash basins and looked into the mirror.

He opened his mouth and started to sing. He could hardly believe it. It was amazing! Brilliant! Fantastic!

'Wow, Ez, what a voice. You're even in tune!'

Eric finished the verse at full throttle and grinned. 'So it's worked then. I'll be OK now. Come on. Let's get back.'

The audience was arriving by the time they reached the stage. Eric waited in the wings, but Wesley went to peer through a hole in the curtain.

'The Mayor's arrived. He's sitting next to Mr Botherington on the front row.'

Eric shrugged. He didn't care now. He knew it was going to be all right.

'Your mum and The Bodge have just arrived,' Wez called a minute later. 'They're heading for the front row, too.'

Eric was glad. He would hate them to miss this performance. It was probably going to be brilliant.

Miss Borrage called, 'Everybody on stage, please.'

All the Bandits and the Mexican Peasants shuffled onto the stage and waited. Mrs Cracker (the Big Cheese) stepped out in front of the curtain to welcome parents to the school. Two minutes passed. The Big Cheese walked off the stage, the piano struck up and the curtains opened.

All went well, Eric thought – except for Kylie Partridge tripping up over a paper-mâché llama, which didn't really count. Before he knew it, the play was almost over. It was time for the last song – and his solo.

The chorus started 'We are the Bandits bold and brave' but Eric didn't join in. He was saving himself. He stood calmly and waited, not wanting to strain his newfound voice. He could see Mum on the front row squirting perfume behind her ears. She was probably nervous for him.

He counted 1 . . . 2 . . . 3 . . . up to 10 and the end of the chorus. He stepped forward ready for his big moment. He glowered at the audience in a dramatic Bandit-like way. He flung back his poncho, spread his arms wide and opened his mouth. But nothing happened.

He coughed to clear his throat and
tried again. Nothing. Not even a croak.
His voice had gone completely. He just
stood and stared down at Mum,
willing her to do something.

To his amazement, she leapt to her

feet. She darted towards the stage and jumped up. Before he knew it, she was there with him. She took a deep breath and began to sing in terrible, high screeching notes. And very loud.

Eric closed his eyes, praying she would stop. But she didn't. She carried on for the full song and, when the chorus joined in, she sang louder than ever. Eric was horrified. But the last straw was seeing his mother pirouette across the stage and curtsy, revealing a huge ladder in her tights. No boy should suffer such embarrassment. It was too much. His knees gave way and everything went black.

Chapter 7

It was amazing! At the party after the show, no one seemed to worry about Eric. No one wondered if he might have a serious disease – or that fainting could prevent him from living a normal, active life.

No. Everyone crowded round Mum, saying how talented she was. Why wasn't she in show business? Eric felt quite depressed. His big moment had vanished into thin air. Mum stood there, surrounded, lapping up all the attention, as if she was some kind of mega star. She smiled. She tossed her head and laughed (very loudly). It was sickening.

'Your mum's a bit weird tonight, isn't she, Ez?' Wesley commented as they stood at the food table. 'She's like a celebrity off the telly.'

Eric nodded gloomily as he reached for the crisps. 'Too much of that lixi-lixi stuff. It has that effect on her. We might have guessed something would go wrong. Auntie Rose's pressies have all been disasters.'

Wez nodded. He knew how it was.

'Mum keeps talking about going into show business,' Eric continued. 'It's really embarrassing. I wish we'd never seen that perfume. And it smells horrible.'

The words had hardly left his lips, when they saw Mum reach into her bag and pull out the very perfume he had mentioned.

'Oh no!' he groaned. 'She's going to use more of the stuff. Things will get worse now. She'll probably climb on the tables and do a dance. I'm off! I can't stand any more.'

'Where're you going, Ez?'

'I'm leaving home. I'll go to London or somewhere.'

'You can't!' said Wez.

'I can,' Eric replied darkly. 'I'll be in touch.' And he headed towards the door. Wesley was gobsmacked. He had to make a move before Eric did something he would regret. He dropped the crisps on the table and charged – head down – into the crowd around Eric's mum. He grabbed her by the knees in a rugby tackle and she rocked back. The bottle shot into the air.

Mum collapsed onto the floor with Wesley beside her.

'WESLEY!' Mrs Robertson shouted. 'WHAT ARE YOU DOING?'

Wesley sat up and looked innocently at his mum.

'Rats,' he said. 'Our school has quite a few. It was going to bite Mrs Braithwaite.'

He didn't care if anyone believed him. He had done what he intended. He had got rid of the perfume. Mrs Braithwaite would soon be her old self and his mate would stay.

Eric came running across the room.

'Are you all right, Mum?' he asked, bending over her. 'Good thing Wez saved you from that rat, eh? It was a big one.'

Mum got to her feet and smiled

warmly at Wesley. Normally she'd be furious. But this was the perfume effect. Still, while she was in this good mood, Eric thought he'd grab the opportunity and ask her again about the holiday.

'You're brilliant, Mum,' he said, handing her a glass of squash. 'Helping me out like that. You deserve a break.'

She looked down with a mumsy expression. 'That would be nice, duck.'

'Can we go on holiday then?'

Her smile slipped a little. 'Not this year, Eric. What with the new baby and everything.'

'But Wez is going to America,' he protested, 'and they've got four kids.'

Wesley's mum, who was standing next to Mrs Braithwaite, raised her eyebrows in surprise.

'America?' she said, turning to her son. 'You keep going on about America, Wesley. You know what I've told you. There's no *chance*. We're going to Blackpool.'

Wez plunged his hands into his pockets and sighed.

'You like the caravan, don't you?' his mum added.

Wez didn't answer. Now he looked even more fed up than Eric.

'I'll tell you what,' said his mum. 'Eric can come, if you like. Your brother says he's too old to go with us this year. So there'll be room for another one.'

Wesley looked at Eric. Eric looked at Wesley. And they grinned broadly.

'A caravan in Blackpool!' said Eric. 'That'll be cool, eh, Wez?'

Just as Eric's holiday was settled at last, something else happened. Everyone noticed a strange smell. Only those who knew Auntie Rose's perfume would recognise it. The bottle, which had been tossed into the air, had splashed the scent onto the radiators and was now giving off a peculiar pong. Everyone stopped what they were doing and sniffed. Then they breathed deeply and said, 'Aaaaah!'

The Big Cheese suddenly became very excited and climbed onto a table.

'Now then,' she said. 'Just to celebrate a wonderful performance, shall we all sing "We are the Bandits bold and brave"?'

Everyone in the room cheered and shouted, YES! (including the Mayor, Mr Botherington, the Chairman of the School Governors and Annie Barnstable's gran). They all sang loud enough to raise the roof and even Eric

found his voice again. They sang it three times with great gusto. It could probably be heard half way across the town.

Only when the perfume faded did everything settle back to normal.

'Isn't it amazing that people can sing so well,' said Mum afterwards. 'You wouldn't believe it, would you?'

The Bodge agreed.

Eric and Wesley exchanged a knowing glance. Only they knew the truth of it.